WENDY ROUILLARD

BARNABY Goes to School

Cartwheel BOOKS®

SCHOLASTIC INC.
New York Toronto London Auckland Sydney
Mexico City New Delhi Hong Kong Buenos Aires

For Mom

To Parents and Educators

Character education teaches children to develop skills and values that enhance their awareness of themselves and others and to use this information to solve real problems and to make good decisions. In each Barnaby book, Barnaby and his friends deal with a variety of character education issues. Through experiences at school and at home, they learn the importance of honesty, self-discipline, empathy, respect, and more — just as young children you know are doing now. By discussing the elements of character education experienced by Barnaby in each book, and by using the suggestions below, you can make the Barnaby books a tool in the character education of children.

In *Barnaby Goes to School*, Barnaby exhibits **courage** and **empathy**. He confronts his fear of starting school (demonstrating **courage**), and he reaches out to befriend a shy girl in his classroom (demonstrating **empathy**).

Parents can help build **courage** by allowing children to take reasonable risks, making the transition from home to school easier. Confidence builds **courage**. Parents can help children feel confident in their abilities to reach out and make friends by providing opportunities for play with other children.

One characteristic of a successful learner is the ability to have insight into the feelings and behaviors of others and to be able to communicate this understanding. When this — **empathy** — is encouraged in children, they are able to develop better friendships. Teachers and parents can help by modeling empathetic speech and actions. Another way to help children develop **empathy** is to help them focus on their own feelings. Once children understand their own thoughts and emotions, they are better able to understand those of others.

To help a child through the first day of school, parents can send a note or a picture from home in the special envelope that comes with this book. A little love from home can go a long way!

Janice Yelland, M.Ed.
Educational Consultant

ISBN 0-439-33306-7

Text and illustrations copyright © 2002 by Wendy Rouillard. All rights reserved.
Published by Scholastic Inc. SCHOLASTIC, CARTWHEEL BOOKS, and associated logos
are trademarks and/or registered trademarks of Scholastic Inc.
Bartlett Farm cookies is used with permission by Bartlett Farm, Nantucket, Massachusetts.

12 11 10 9 8 7 6 5 4 3 2 1   02 03 04 05 06

Printed in China 62 • First Scholastic printing, August 2002

On a faraway land, many miles out to sea,
Lives a cute, young bear named Barnaby.
He is sweet and adorable and cuddly, too.
He may be a bear, but he's like me and you.

Now Barnaby's off! School is starting today.
There is much to be learned as he goes on his way.
At first he'll be scared, but soon he'll feel better,
Thanks to a friend and a very special letter.

Barnaby loved an adventure.

skiing the Colorado Rockies,

and traveling to faraway places.

He wanted to be a world-famous explorer when he grew up.

He loved exploring the seashore,

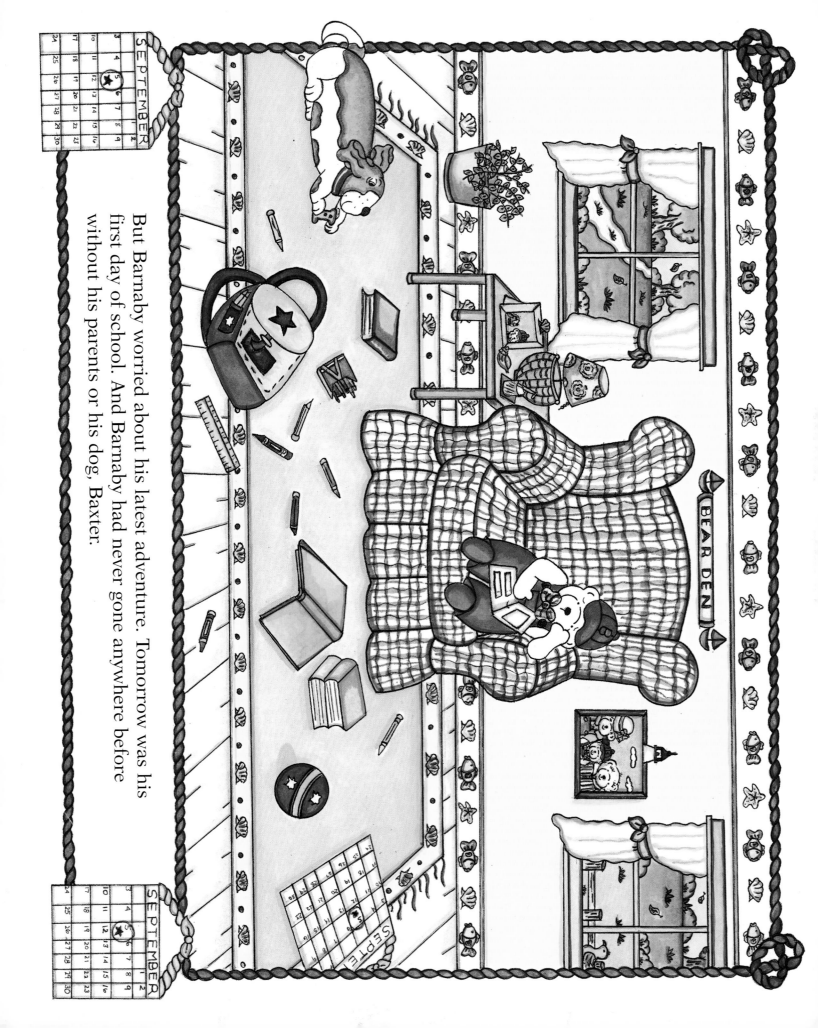

But Barnaby worried about his latest adventure. Tomorrow was his first day of school. And Barnaby had never gone anywhere before without his parents or his dog, Baxter.

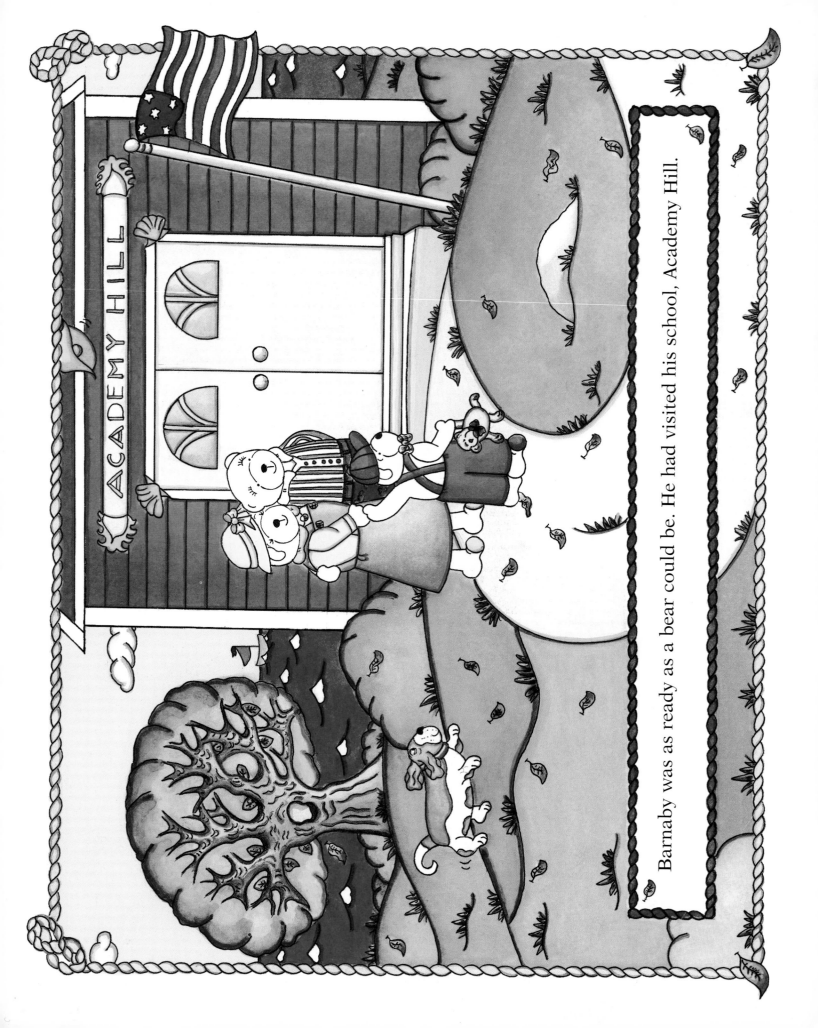

Barnaby was as ready as a bear could be. He had visited his school, Academy Hill.

He'd met Mrs. Sealey, his teacher.

He'd met Hector, the school boat driver.

But Barnaby still worried.

Barnaby didn't understand why he even had to go to school. At home there were plenty of adventures to keep him busy.

"I wish I could stay home with you," said Barnaby.
"I wish I could go to school with you," said Baxter.

"What if I can't find anyone to play with me?" asked Barnaby. "What if Mrs. Sealey is mean to me?" "Go with the flow and don't worry so much," said his mother. "Barnaby, you're a very special bear. I know you'll be fine."

"Just fine," said his father.
But Barnaby didn't feel just fine.

and combed his fur.

brushed his teeth,

Early the next morning Barnaby got dressed,

His mother prepared his favorite breakfast: hot Morning Glory muffins with beach plum jam. Barnaby ate slowly. He knew that when he finished, it would be time to go.

Side by side, Barnaby and his parents walked to the school boat stop. Barnaby wore his sporty new backpack, specially designed to help handle any new adventure. It was filled with all the necessary supplies: a brand-new box of crayons, sharpened pencils, and a pad of paper.

Barnaby could see the boat up ahead.
He knew he didn't have much time.

"I just realized," said Barnaby. "I can't go to school.
Baxter has never been alone before. He won't eat
unless I give him his food. And he won't go for
a walk unless I take him."

"I'll take care of Baxter,"
said Barnaby's mother.

"He'll be just fine,
And so will you," said Barnaby's father.
But Barnaby didn't feel just fine.

"Ahoy there, mates! Hop on board the school boat express," shouted Hector.

Barnaby boarded at the bow of the boat and waved good-bye. The school boat went *bumpidy-bumpidy splash.* Gigantic knots tugged and twisted in Barnaby's tummy.

School can't be that hard, thought Barnaby. Certainly not harder than climbing Mount Everest. Or parachuting out of an airplane. Or even sailing across the Atlantic Ocean. These were adventures that Barnaby dreamed about. But of course, he had never dreamed of traveling alone.

When Barnaby arrived at Academy Hill, the classroom was bustling with activity. His classmates scrambled to find their name tags, searched for their cubbies, and unloaded their backpacks. Huge maps decorated the walls, paper animals hung from the ceiling, and a colorful rug covered the floor.

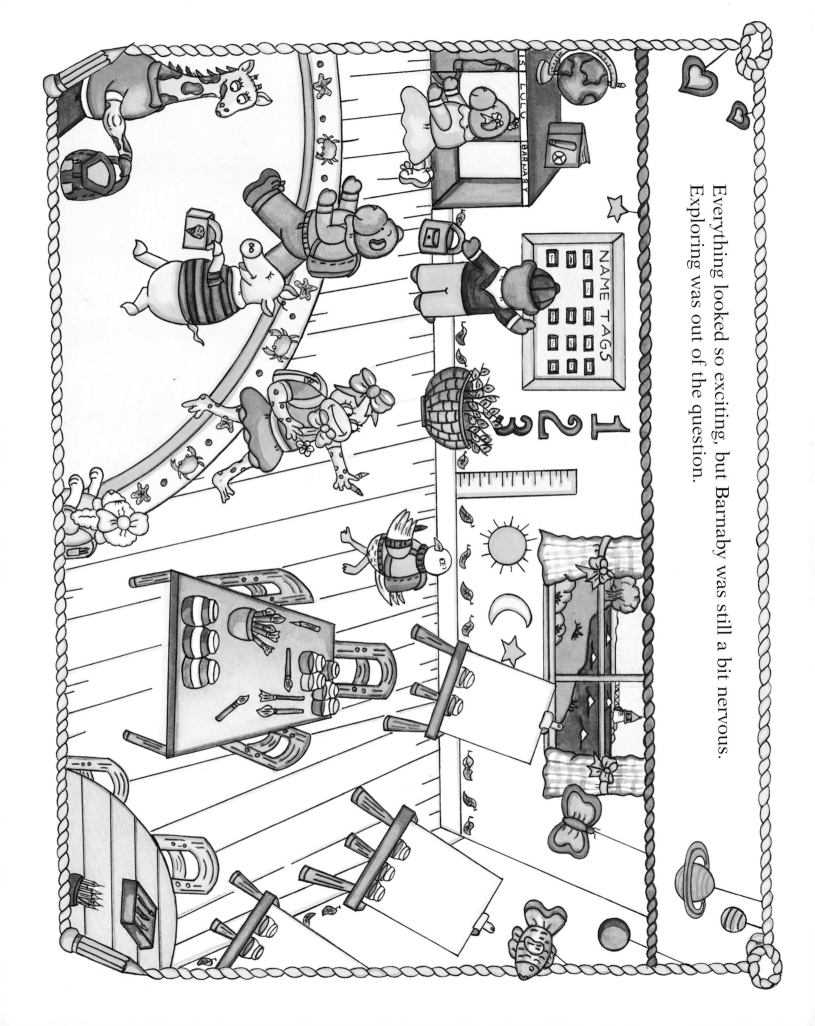

Everything looked so exciting, but Barnaby was still a bit nervous. Exploring was out of the question.

"Welcome, welcome!" Mrs. Sealey sang. "Let's gather around in a circle. Tell everyone your name and a little something about yourself."

"Hi, I'm Ellery.
I love to ride my scooter,
play the drums, and eat
peanut butter cookies!"

"My name is Freda, but you can call me Fancy Freda. I love to dress in fancy clothes and dance around my bedroom in my mommy's high heels!"

"Hi, my name is Jimmy. I'm a super-duper soccer player. I love to tell jokes, and my favorite food is cheese because it makes everything taste better."

"My name is Bar…"

Barnaby froze. He was scared speechless.

What if everyone makes fun of what I say? What if everyone thinks I'm weird because I have red paw pads? What if…?

"Barnaby, would you like us to come back to you in a few minutes?" asked Mrs. Sealey in a soft voice.

Barnaby nodded and stuck both paws deep into his pockets. To his surprise, he pulled out a small white envelope. Inside there was a note.

Luckily, Barnaby had practiced reading. He could read every word his parents had written.

DEAR BARNABY,
YOU ARE A VERY SPECIAL BEAR!
I KNOW YOU WILL BE FINE.
LOVE, ♥ MOMMY
JUST FINE.
xoxo DADDY
🐾 BAXTER

Barnaby felt much better. He tucked the note safely into the top pocket of his overalls. Then he raised his paw.

"Are you ready now?" asked Mrs. Sealey.

Barnaby nodded.

"My name is Barnaby. I love to explore on my bicycle. I take really good care of my dog, Baxter. In the summer, I like to pick beach plums and make beach plum jam."

Everyone smiled.

Circle time was over now. As Barnaby stood up he noticed that the girl who was sitting next to him had been too shy to speak.

"What's your name?" asked Barnaby.
"My name is Baisley," she said.

"My name starts with a B just like your name," said Barnaby.

"My name ends with a Y just like your name," said Baisley.

"I have red paw pads," said Barnaby.
"Look! I have red paw pads, too!" said Baisley.

"I have a few jitters," whispered Barnaby.
"Me, too!" whispered Baisley.

Barnaby and Baisley spent the entire day together going from one activity to another.

Then they went to the art corner.

First they played outside in the sandbox.

And in the afternoon, they played market.

After lunch, they sat together at story time.

Mrs. Sealey was very friendly. She was always there to answer questions or help out. And she served the most delicious snack: Bartlett Farm cookies with cranberries and chocolate chips — Barnaby's favorite and Baisley's, too!

Barnaby kept the note from his parents close to his heart just in case he began to feel lonely. But he never needed to look at it again — not even one more time.

The first day of school whizzed by. It was great! And the best part of all was that Barnaby made a brand-new friend.

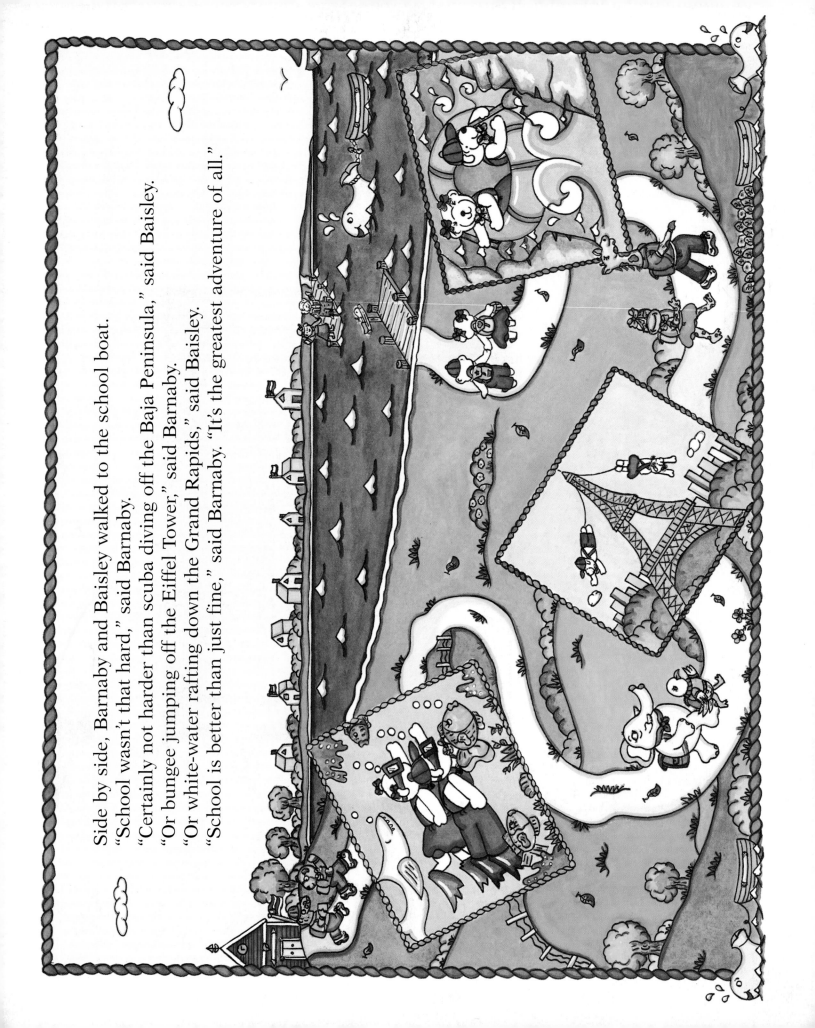

Side by side, Barnaby and Baisley walked to the school boat.

"School wasn't that hard," said Barnaby.

"Certainly not harder than scuba diving off the Baja Peninsula," said Baisley.

"Or bungee jumping off the Eiffel Tower," said Barnaby.

"Or white-water rafting down the Grand Rapids," said Baisley.

"School is better than just fine," said Barnaby. "It's the greatest adventure of all."